Pete the Cat

Construction Destruction

Harperfestival is an imprint of HarperCollins Publishers.
Pete the Cat: Construction Destruction
Copyright © 2015 by James Dean. All rights reserved.
Manufactured in China.

For information address HarperCollins Children's Books, a division of HarperCollins Publishers,
195 Broadway, New York, NY 10007.
www.harpercollinschildrens.com
Library of Congress catalog card number: 2014949449
ISBN 978-0-06-269916-9
17 18 19 20 21   SCP   10 9 8 7 6 5 4 3 2 1
❖
First Edition

Pete the Cat

Construction Destruction

by James Dean

HARPER FESTIVAL
An Imprint of HarperCollinsPublishers

"Recess!" Pete shouts as the bell rings. But when Pete gets outside to play—oh no. The playground is a disaster. The swings are broken, the slide is rusty, and the sandbox is full of weeds.

Pete makes plans for a new playground.
"Wow!" says Principal Nancy. "Can you really build that?"
"Not by myself," says Pete. "I'm going to need some help."
"Whatever you need, Pete, it's yours."

PLANS for NEW PLAYGROUND
By PETE the Cat

Rumble! Rumble! Honk!

The next day, Pete arrives at the playground before school. The construction crew is already there. He gives them the go-ahead to tear down the old playground.

Creak! Crash!

Down goes the slide.

Clink! Clank!

Down go the swings.

Bang! Boom! Down goes the tower.

Honk! Honk! A truck arrives to recycle the metal.

The new playground equipment has arrived. It's time to get to work. The cement mixer will pour concrete. The dump truck will bring sand and dirt. The backhoe will dig. The whole team will get the job done.

Building a playground is hard work.

The new playground is cool, but it's not cool enough.
"What do you think?" Pete asks, holding up his latest plans.
"It will be too hard to build," says one of the workers.
"And everything is almost finished," says another.

"But it will make this the best playground ever," Pete says.
"Then let's do it," the workers say.

Screwdrivers twist in screws. Wrenches tighten the nuts. The workers try to make everything perfect.

Hooray!

The new playground is ready.

Everyone is amazed, until . . .

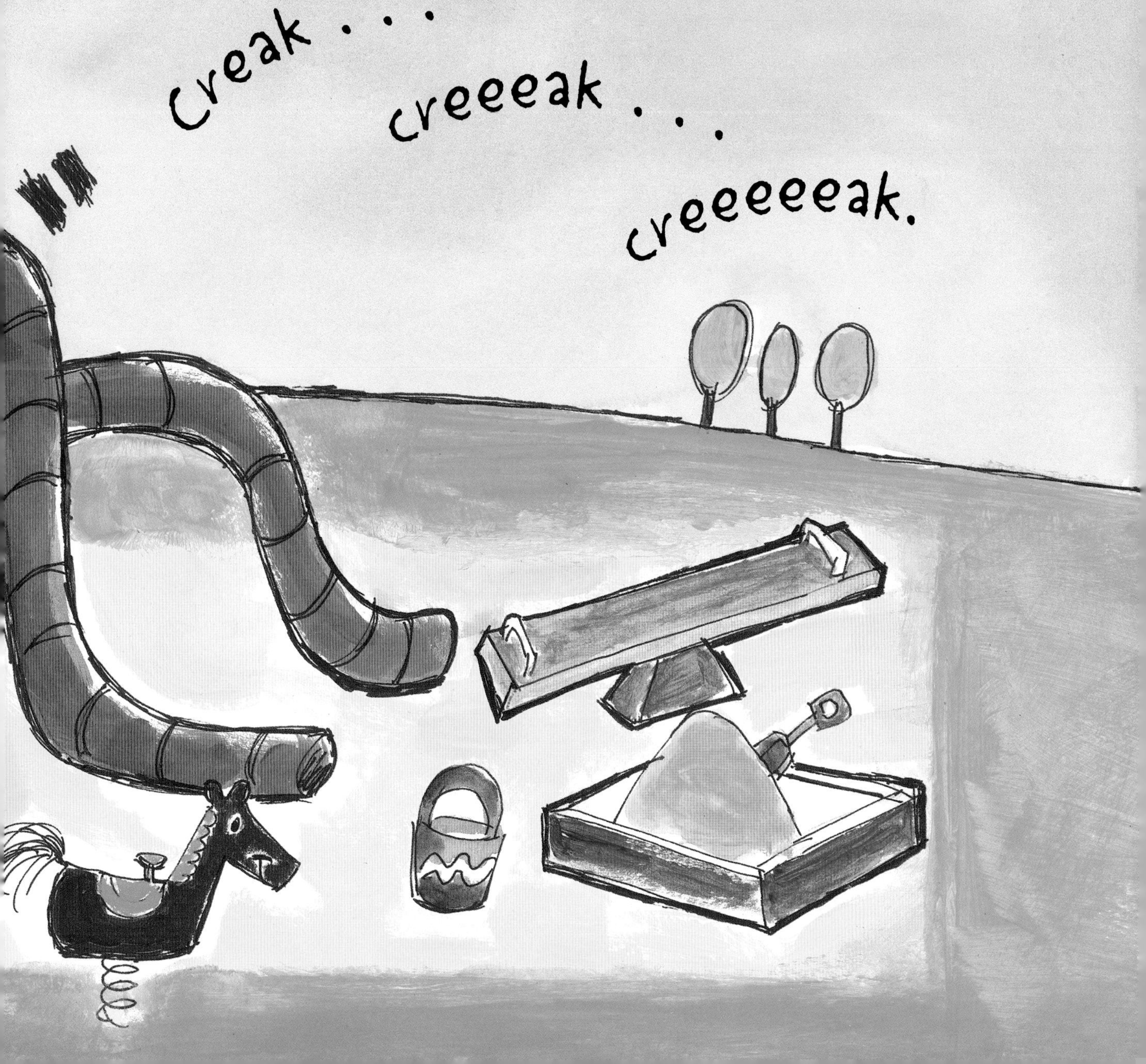

Smash! Crunch! Thud!

"Oh no!" says Principal Nancy as the new playground crashes to the ground. "The pieces are all mixed up."

Everyone is disappointed—except for Pete.

"It's not how we planned it!" Pete shouts.
"It's even better!"

This playground is filled with surprises and places to explore. The school playground is the most amazing playground ever.

Sometimes you've got to dare to dream big.

Pete the Cat

Cavecat Pete

by James Dean

HARPER FESTIVAL
An Imprint of HarperCollins Publishers

Harperfestival is an imprint of HarperCollins Publishers.

Pete the Cat: Cavecat Pete
Library of Congress catalog card number: 2014945515
ISBN 978-0-06-269915-2

Book design by Jeanne Hogle
17 18 19 20 21   SCP   10 9 8 7 6 5 4 3 2 1

First Edition

Cavecat Pete wakes up early. The sun is shining. The birds are singing.

Today is going to be a great day, Pete thinks. But then Pete's bed starts to shake. His friend Vinny the Velociraptor is coming to visit.

"It's a perfect day for a picnic!" says Vinny.

"What a great idea," says Pete. "Who should we invite?"

"Everyone!" Vinny yells.

"Right on!" says Pete.

Pete loves picnics! He heads out to invite all his friends.

First Pete finds his good friend
Ethel the Apatosaurus!
To get her attention, Pete climbs
all the way up to the top of the
tallest tree.

"Would you like to come to a picnic?" Pete asks.
"I'd love to," says Ethel. "What can I bring?"
"How about a really big salad?" Pete suggests.
"What a great idea," says Ethel. "I'm on it!"

Pete wanders along the river. He sees T. rex!
T. rex plays guitar. T. rex is awesome!

"Hey, T. rex," Pete yells, "want to come to a
picnic?"

"Sweet," says T. rex. "Can I bring my guitar?"

"Definitely," says Pete. "We can jam!"

"Count me in," says T. rex. "Okay if I bring
Al the Allosaurus? He's a whiz on the drums."

"The more the merrier," says Pete.

Pete sees his friend Terri the Pterosaur in the sky.
"Hi, Pete!" she calls.

Pete invites Terri to the picnic, too. "Would you mind giving me a lift?" Pete asks.
"Sure," says Terri. "Climb aboard."

Pete sees the spiked tail of his main man Skip the Stegosaurus.

"How are you feeling today, Skip?" Pete asks. Skip has been sick with the sniffles.

"Better," says Skip. "Thanks for asking."

"You up for a picnic?"

"I think so," says Skip. "I'd hate to miss the fun."

It's almost time for the picnic! Cavecat Pete rushes through the forest. He doesn't want to be late. Whoops! Pete trips over Trini the Triceratops.

"We're playing hide-and-seek," she says before Pete can ask what she was doing. "I think I hid a little too well."

"How long have you been there?" asks Pete.

"What's today?" asks Trini.

"Well, all the dinosaurs are going to be at the picnic grounds. Want to come?" Pete asks.

"What a great idea! Maybe somebody there will play hide-and-seek with me!"

It's time for the picnic. Vinny and Ethel are setting up the picnic tables. T. rex and Al are warming up to play some tunes. Terri and Trini are playing hide-and-seek. Even Skip seems to be enjoying himself!

"It doesn't get any better than this," Pete says.

T. rex comes over then. "Hey, Pete," he asks, "is there anything else to eat? I'm a carnivore. I don't eat salad."

Trini comes over. "Terri is cheating at hide-and-seek. She's flying around and peeking."

Skip comes over. "I don't feel so good," he says, and he sneezes.

The dinosaurs all start to argue. The picnic will be ruined if Pete doesn't do something. He leans over to Al and says, "Can you give me a beat?" Pete takes out his guitar, and he starts to sing.

Before long, everyone is having a great time.
"You know," T. rex tells Ethel, "I've never
actually tried salad before."
"Try it," says Pete. "I bet you'll like it."

T. rex tastes the salad. Crunch, crunch, crunch.
"Yum!" says T. rex. "This salad is delicious!"
Everyone grabs a plate and digs in.

Everyone decides to play hide-and-seek.
Pete is happy that everyone is getting along.
He feels lucky to have such great friends.

"This was the best picnic ever," everyone agrees.

"It was the best picnic because you guys are the best friends ever," Pete says.

And no one can argue with that.

Pete the Cat

Robo-Pete

by James Dean

HARPER FESTIVAL
An Imprint of HarperCollins Publishers

Harperfestival is an imprint of HarperCollins Publishers.

Pete the Cat: Robo-Pete
Copyright © 2015 by James Dean. All rights reserved.
Manufactured in China.
No part of this book may be used or reproduced in any manner whatsoever without written permission
except in the case of brief quotations embodied in critical articles and reviews.
For information address HarperCollins Children's Books, a division of HarperCollins Publishers,
195 Broadway, New York, NY 10007.
www.harpercollinschildrens.com

Library of Congress Control Number: 2015936663
ISBN 978-0-06-269919-0

Book design by Jeanne Hogle
17 18 19 20 21   SCP   10 9 8 7 6 5 4 3 2 1
❖
First Edition

What a great, sunny morning!
Pete can't wait to play baseball
with his friends.

"Do you want to play catch?"
Pete asks Larry.
   "I can't," says Larry.
"I'm going to the library."

"Do you want to play catch?"
Pete asks Callie.
   "I was about to go for a
bike ride," says Callie.

"Do you want to play catch?" Pete asks John.
"I can't right now," says John. "I have to paint the fence."

Pete wishes his friends would do what he wants to do. It's no fun playing catch all by himself.
If only I knew another me . . . , Pete thinks. And like that, Pete has a great idea!

Pete builds a robot! He programs it to be just like him.

"Welcome to the world, Robo-Pete!" Pete says to the robot.
"You're my new best friend. We'll do everything together."

"And I want to play catch," says Pete.
"Great idea!" says Robo-Pete.

Pete and Robo-Pete play catch.

"Wow!" says Pete, running after the ball. "You sure can throw far!"

Robo-Pete throws farther and farther until . . .

"Time out!" says Pete as he tries to catch his breath.
"Let's play something else."
  "I want to play whatever you want to play,"
Robo-Pete says proudly.

"How about we play hide-and-seek?" says Pete.
"That will be fun," says Robo-Pete.

Pete finds the best hiding place ever! He's sure Robo-Pete will never find him.

"Ten, nine, eight, seven, six, five, four, three, two, one!" shouts Robo-Pete. "Ready or not, here I come!"

"Gotcha!" shouts Robo-Pete, tagging Pete.
"Hey, how did you find me?" says Pete.
"With my homing device," says Robo-Pete.
"I can find anyone, anywhere."

"Okay, enough hide-and-seek," says Pete. "Let's play some guitar."

Pete teaches Robo-Pete how to play a song he made up.

"You have to feel the music,"
Pete explains.
"Okay," says Robo-Pete.

"To feel it, I need to play loud," explains Robo-Pete.

Pete tries to stop Robo-Pete, but Robo-Pete
can't hear him over the noise. . . .

"This is fun," says Robo-Pete.

"This is awful!" says Pete the Cat.

"Okay," says Robo-Pete. "Let's ride our skateboards instead."

Before Pete can answer, Robo-Pete's feet transform into a motorized skateboard with super speedy wheels.

"Let's go!"

Robo-Pete shouts.

"Wait!" calls Pete.

Pete chases after Robo-Pete. He has no idea where Robo-Pete is going.

Robo-Pete crashes into the sandbox at the playground.
"Are you okay?" Pete asks his robot.

"I am a robot. I am indestructible!" says Robo-Pete.
"What is this strange place?"
"It's a playground," says Pete. He waves to his friends.

"This is Robo-Pete," Pete says to Callie, Larry, and John.
"I made him myself."
"Cool," says Larry.

"We are going to help John finish painting," says Callie.
"And then we are going bike riding."
"I want to go on the slide!" interrupts Robo-Pete.

"Robo-Pete, I want to help my friends paint the fence!"
Pete tells his robot.

"Paint the fence—that would be great," Robo-Pete says.
"I am programmed to paint faster than anyone."

Pete and his friends try to help, but Robo-Pete paints too fast.

So instead they ride bikes,

and they read books . . .

and after Robo-Pete is done painting,
they help him clean the brushes.

Pete realizes that it doesn't matter what they do.
Just being with his friends is what makes it fun!

Pete the Cat

Go, Pete, Go!

by James Dean

HARPER FESTIVAL

An Imprint of HarperCollinsPublishers

Harperfestival is an imprint of HarperCollins Publishers.

Pete the Cat: Go, Pete, Go!

For information address HarperCollins Children's Books, a division of HarperCollins Publishers,
195 Broadway, New York, NY 10007.
www.harpercollinschildrens.com

Library of Congress Control Number: 2015952439
ISBN 978-0-06-269918-3

The artist used pen and ink, with watercolor and acrylic paint,
on 300lb hot press paper to create the illustrations for this book.

17 18 19 20 21   SCP   10 9 8 7 6 5 4 3 2 1

❖

First Edition

It's a beautiful day, and Pete the Cat has decided to take his bike for a ride. Nothing makes Pete happier than feeling the sun on his fur and the breeze on his face.

Vroom! Vroom!

Turtle has a new race car. "Who wants to have a race?" he says.

"Not me," says Grumpy Toad.
"My motorcycle has a flat tire."

"Not me," says Emma.
"My car is too old and slow."

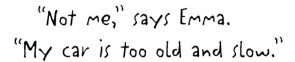

"Not me," says Callie.
"My bus is a work of art.
It's not meant for racing."

"I'll race you," says Pete, knowing how much Turtle likes to race.

"But your bike has no motor," says Turtle. "My race car is super quick. I'll win for sure."

"That's okay," says Pete. "I just want to try my best and have fun."

Everyone is excited for the big race.

"On your mark. Get set. Go!" Callie shouts.

Turtle steps on the gas pedal and—vroom!—zooms away.

Pete waves good-bye
and then pedals off.

Pete sees Turtle up ahead. Turtle slows
down to let Pete catch up.

"Check this out!"

shouts Turtle. He presses a button and . . .

... Fins appear!

Now Turtle's race car goes even faster.

Vrrroom! Vrrroom!

Pete's bike doesn't have fins, but he does have a basket.
He stops and takes out a tasty red apple.

Nothing is better than a tasty red apple on a beautiful day.

Turtle sees that Pete is WAY behind. He spies a diner up ahead. "Might as well grab a bite to eat," Turtle says as he pulls into a parking spot.

"Yum!" says Turtle, eating a grilled-cheese sandwich. He is in no rush. He is sure he will win the race.

"Dessert?" the waitress asks. "Don't mind if I do," Turtle says.

While Turtle finishes his lunch, Pete continues pedaling. The sun is high and the breeze is blowing. It's a beautiful day for a race.

Pete sees Turtle leaving the diner. Pete waves hello, but Turtle doesn't wave back. Turtle just jumps in his car and peels off.

"I guess he didn't see me." Pete shrugs.

But Turtle did see Pete. He knows that Pete isn't going to give up easily.

So Turtle presses a button and his tires inflate into mag wheels that let him swerve around the curves at top speed!

vrrr-vrrr-vrrroooom!

Pete passes a rosebush as he goes around a curve. Pete knows he should keep racing, but he can't resist.

The roses are just so beautiful. . . . He has to stop to smell them.

Turtle sees that he has a HUGE lead.
He knows he's going to win.

LEMONADE

He stops for a nice,
cold glass of lemonade, and that's when
he sees the hammock hanging between
two trees. He's exhausted from racing so fast.
He figures a quick nap will help him in the home stretch.

Pete pedals past and sees Turtle sleeping. That's cool, Pete thinks as he rides by as quietly as he can. "Turtle must really be tired. I'm glad he's getting some rest."

Grumpy Toad finds Turtle fast asleep!

"Wake up, Turtle," says Grumpy Toad. "If you don't get back in the race, Pete is going to win."

"That's impossible," says Turtle,
thinking it must be a joke.
But it's no joke!

Turtle presses a button and rocket boosters appear, making him go super-duper fast.

Vrrrrrrooooooooooooooom!

FINISH

But by the time Turtle nears the finish line . . .

. . . Pete has already won the race!

"How did you do it?" Turtle asks.
"Slow and steady," says Pete. "Maybe next
time instead of racing, we can ride together."
"Great idea," says Turtle.

Pete the Cat
and the Treasure Map

by
James Dean

ARPER FESTIVAL
An Imprint of HarperCollins Publishers

Harperfestival is an imprint of HarperCollins Publishers.

Pete the Cat and the Treasure Map
Copyright © 2017 by James Dean
All rights reserved. Manufactured in China.

Library of Congress Control Number: 2016938983
ISBN 978-0-06-269914-5

The artist used pen and ink, with watercolor and acrylic paint,
on 300lb hot press paper to create the illustrations for this book.

17 18 19 20 21   SCP   10 9 8 7 6 5 4 3 2 1
❖
First Edition

Captain Pete looks across Cat Cove. The sun is sparkling
on the water. It's a beautiful day for an adventure!
Something flies toward Captain Pete's ship. It's a parrot!

"Squawk!" says the parrot. She gives Captain Pete a crumpled piece of paper.
"What is it?" asks First Mate Callie.

Captain Pete looks at the paper. There's a long trail that ends with an X. "It's a treasure map!" he says.

"Treasure!" says First Mate Callie. "Where?"

"On Secret Island," says Captain Pete.

"Let's go!" says First Mate Callie.

"Woo-hoo!" cries the crew. "Treasure!"

Captain Pete steers the ship through the big waves. The salty wind pushes the sails. The ship is going really fast.

"Good job, mateys," says Captain Pete.
"We'll be there in no time!"

Uh-oh. Captain Pete spoke too soon.
He spies something coming toward them.
"What is that?" asks First Mate Callie.

A giant arm reaches up and splashes the water.
It makes a wave that crashes down on Pete's boat.

KRR-SPLASH!

"Squawk," cries the parrot.

"Arrrrrgh!" yells the crew.

KRR-SPLASH! Another arm comes crashing down.

The crew is scared, but not Captain Pete.
He knows that the monster isn't trying to scare
them. He's rocking a cool beat.

Captain Pete takes out his guitar and strums. The monster rises out of the water. The crew takes cover, but the monster stops when he hears Pete playing.

He nods his head along. He's not a scary sea monster—
he's an awesome sea drummer!

"Rock on!" says Captain Pete.
"Thanks!" booms the monster.

"Oh no, captain!" shouts First Mate Callie. "A big storm is coming!"

"Batten down the hatches!" says Captain Pete. Everyone gets ready for the storm.

The waves toss the ship, but the crew is brave.

Captain Pete has an idea. "Hey there, Friend!" he yells to the sea monster. "We need some help."

The monster grabs the ship with his giant arms and gives it a great big boost.

The ship moves right through the storm!

"Hooray!" shouts the crew as the monster swims up to the boat.

"Thanks, friend!" yells Captain Pete.
"No problem," booms the monster.

"Land ho!" yells First Mate Callie, pointing out over the sea. All the pirates rush to look.

"It's Secret Island!" says Captain Pete.

On the beach, their buddy Grumpy Toad is waiting with a glittering pile of treasure!

"Ahoy, mateys. You got my map!" Grumpy Toad says. "Treasure is no fun if you can't share it with your friends."

The crew is so happy, they do cat-wheels in the sand.
"Thanks, Grumpy Toad!" they shout.

"I think we're missing something," says Captain Pete.
"Let's play some music!"

"What a great idea!"
says Grumpy Toad.

The pirates load all the treasure onto the ship.
Captain Pete takes out his guitar and strums. But
something is missing from his song. . . .

"Our drummer," Captain Pete says as the sea monster pops his head above the waves. "Would you like to join my crew?"

"AYE!" booms the monster.

"Rock on!" Captain Pete says as the monster joins in on a rockin' pirate tune.

Captain Pete's crew is complete. All the pirates sing,

"Yo ho, yo ho, a pirate's life for us!"